Quantum Entanglement

Unforsaken Grimm

Volume 15

Ralph K Jones

Table of Contents

Sacrifice 1

Synergy 6

Arena...10

Two Minds...14

The Lust for That at Peace......................................18

Gatekeepers..23

Protectors...26

A Small Distraction..31

Broken but Stronger...34

Taste by Design...37

About The Author..40

Continue Your Journey..41

Sacrifice

Sacrifice

The military unit had taken heavy casualties, stranded on an alien world and fighting a creature unlike anything any of them had seen before. They were low on ammo and even lower on options. This was not like a regular conflict and some manner of strategy or trickery was needed. Lesko looked to his men, desperate for options.

"I might be able to be of some help, sir," a young soldier came as he set down a large piece of paper on the ground from his pack.

Other soldiers began to hold the position as he began to sketch things.

"I am a tactical sniper officer and it is my job to lay out a battlefield and figure out the angles. I can assume from where I have seen the thing attack at us to be its range. Whenever one of us tries to leave its range it attacks more aggressively to keep us in. Therefore, it is a simple matter to find a central point within all of the attack points to figure out where it is. The creature seems to be in this area here, by the well behind where the trader led us. I would almost ensure that it is down in that well."

"That thing is not going to let us get closer to that well," another soldier stated. "It is going to throw everything it has at us."

"I know," Lesko replied. "But this is the only way. We do not know why we were brought here, and we don't know by who. One thing I do know is that too many of us have fallen to this thing and that I for one will not allow us all to fall to this stupid alien. We are going to all attack it as one and we are going to kill it!"

The men all cheered, focusing on what was ahead and what had
to be done.

Lesko's impromptu unit rallied behind him, they knew that even
with him there that the field was wrought with danger, but they
did not care. They charged behind him, taking heavy losses but
using every advantage he could buy for them.

For the first time in the conflict, the human soldiers gained
ground against the monster, pushing back and taking the front
line. The soldiers were not really worrying about themselves,
focusing on getting Lesko and the bomber to the well so they
could finish it.

Lesko knew they could not easily win in this matter but the only
chance they had was this last-ditch bold manoeuvre. They had to
show their captors that they would not fall and they were simply
wasting their time. Lesko knew this was a battle they might not
be able to win, but he would do anything for his men and not
leave them to a horrific fate as long as he drew breath.

The beast for its part was sending its own message. It ran on
terror and knew what effect it had on the morale on the opposing
force. It was powerful, it was in possession of superior strength,
but they were not as powerful as the bravery of the humans.
Should it lose the fear of its power that they held over the others
it became far less oppressive.

Lesko had been stealing the resolves of his men since the
beginning but knew that only his actions now truly motivated
them. In the battle of morale and motivation...he was
clearly winning.

However, in the reality of the battle the force of the beast was
too powerful. They surged forward, piling up the losses the beast
laid upon them. The humans began to fatigue, taking attack after
attack from the beast.

Lesko and the bomb tech made it to the well, the remains of the unit holding back to draw off the beast's attacks. Lesko stood, creating a firing line of skill and savagery as the tech did the final prep to the bomb. He stood up lifting it to throw over the side. A tentacle came from nowhere, snatching the man and lifting him into the air. It began to crush his body into a paste and as his last act he let go of the bomb, letting it fall in front of Lesko.

The commander dropped his weapon, scrambling to pick up the bomb before it went off. He tossed it over the side into the well and ran into the fray. There was smoke everywhere and he had no weapons left beside a small pistol. There were only a handful of men still standing and it was utter chaos.

A massive explosion went off, shaking the ground, causing many of the buildings to sink beneath the ground into the tunnels dug by the creature. An inhuman death scream came from below, making Lesko's ears ring as he struggled through the smoke and dust. He did not know what he was looking for, and he did not know where he was going.

A strange sound permeated through the chorus of destruction; it sounded like cheering. It was like thousands of voices cried out in excitement for the battle that had just been won and it made everything seem less real.

A door opened in one of the buildings and there was bright light behind it. Lesko walked through it, not knowing what else he should do.

Beyond was a myriad of workers, all seeming to be dealing with equipment like the behind the scenes area of a sporting game. It seemed that the world that seemed so real was only a stage, one that he and his men had fallen for wholeheartedly and died in. He walked past the workers, knowing that they would not have

the answers he sought. He ended up in a control room of sorts
with a portly man sitting amidst a sea of monitors.

Lesko was shocked...it all felt so real, the pain, the danger, the
death...the battle was a farce and the only reality to it was the
blood spilled by those who followed him.

Synergy

Synergy

S ubject had never really been in a fight before—at least, nothing that had been more than a little skirmish between rivals. However, as he moved through the guards that were coming after him, he felt mighty and he felt a certain thrill in the battle.

He was different now. There was something in him that had awoken by the genetic tampering, and now that it was awake, he could not put it back to sleep again.

He was much faster than the guards and police officers, going between them and striking them so hard that few could take more than one hit. The tasers stung at him but the more he got hit by them the more he got used to it. It was as if his body was rigged to survive at all costs; the strange genes activating within him making him strong enough to face anything.

However, as powerful as he was, as strong as he was, there was one simple fact...he was outnumbered. He knew that it was only a matter of time before one of the cops decided to use their guns, even with the fear of hurting the other men around it.

Subject felt power like never before but knew that he was still mostly a man and that his energy would run out. He could already feel fatigue deep inside; the rage and instinct that fueled him struggling to stay alert and absolute.

That is when he saw her, a solitary woman, fighting with the same speed and strength that he had. She had come in from the other side, flanking the guards and police, punching through them in a mad swath to get to him. He did not know who she was, but he knew somehow that she was just like him. She was a genetic abnormality and whatever she wanted from him was a hell of a lot better than what he imagined the doctors inside had in store for him.

This newcomer gave him purpose and drive and it focused Subject on a course of action and he got his second wind. He focused not just on blind fighting but to fight his way to the woman.

Within moments he was side by side with her and they instinctively went back to back. Without having to worry about all around him, Subject found it easier going. He and the newcomer worked together and soon enough there were no more guards or cops standing to oppose them.

"Who are you?" Subject asked. "Are you like me?"

"I am," the woman answered. "I am Hunter. We need to focus on getting out of here."

Subject nodded and as Hunter took off running, he was right at her heels. She seemed to know her way out and Subject was glad for it. They attacked any guards that stood in their way, moving fast and trying not to get bogged down. Subject wondered why the alarm had gone silent. He had not noticed it had done so but one moment it was on, the next moment it was not. It seemed like Hunter had indeed come for him and it was a rescue

Things were moving so fast for Subject that his head spun as he tried to compartmentalise it all. He shook it off. There would be time for questions to be answered later; survival came first.

Soon Hunter and Subject were away from the facility, holding up in an under-construction building.

Waiting for them was a slim woman who looked like she had just gotten there.

"This is Scout," Hunter explained. "There are only three of us together now but there are many more people out there like us. Will you help us find them...will you help us protect them?"

"I will," Subject answered with no hesitation. "I don't want anyone to have to go through what I did if they don't have to."

"Good," Hunter said with a nod. "Because we are at war and being so...we will need more warriors."

Arena

Arena

Lesko stood in a strange facility, surrounded by coverage like it was a sporting event. He was shocked; it felt so real and he had no end of questions.

The man running the terminals looked up to Lesko with an apologetic face. "You need to understand; you are not meant to see any of this.

"...Why?" Lesko managed. "Why did you do this?"

"For ratings, silly," the control man replied nonchalantly. "A question was posted on the boards to whether an elite unit of human soldiers from the twenty-first century could find a Death Grasper. So, we did what we did and made it happen. I do not mind telling you that we had a packed house and viewership was through the roof.

"This was all for entertainment?" Lesko asked furiously. "The lives of my men were taken for other people's satisfaction. You ripped us from our lives to perform for you?"

"Well, yes and no," the control man replied. "It was for entertainment, but we did not really...rip you from anywhere. You would be surprised to know it is many, many years after your death and a very, very far away place. You are basically a clone of yourself at your peak."

Lesko struggled with the implications, trying to disprove it but realising that though he had assumed his memories were intact, he seemed to find a lot of glaring holes in it. He wanted to not believe it but was forced to it. He was no one, a clone, built to fight and perform and was nothing. His determination, his bravery, those of his men as well, none of it was real. Inner turmoil flooded over him as he drew his pistol and pointed it at the control man.

"Hey now," the control man said, slightly flustered. "You don't actually think that will work here? We would never give you guns that would hurt the people who they are not supposed to hurt."

"I fought a beast beyond anything I had ever fought before just now," Lesko explained. "And when we assaulted toward the well, I sensed fear in it. If I can see fear in a monster, I can sense it in you. If my gun was rigged to not fire here...you would not be so scared of it."

"It is not me you want to kill anyway!" the control man replied nervously. "It is our benefactor, the man who set all of this up. He is who you want to kill."

"I would imagine my chances of getting to him are rather slim." Lesko replied.

"Probably," the control man conceded.

"Then you will have to do," Lesko replied as he pulled the trigger, shooting the man in the head; killing him instantly and causing him to slump over his control boards.

Lesko sheathed his gun, turned around and walked back toward the pitch. He did not know what would happen next, what would await him. But all he could do is find out who in his unit still lived and see what could be done for them. They might not all be real, but their commitment to each other still was.

"That was an amazing fight," a voice said over the intercom. "One of the best I have seen in a long time."

"I would presume you are the benefactor of all this?" Lesko asked.

"Indeed," the benefactor replied. "Do not worry about the content manager you just shot. He was nobody really."

"So, what of us?" Lesko asked. "What now?"

"You understand there is nowhere for you to go back to, right?" the benefactor asked rhetorically. "That this is your world now?"

"Yes," Lesko replied.

"Then could I talk you into more battles?" the benefactor inquired. "The crowd loved you."

"Two conditions," Lesko insisted. "And we will fight again."

"Anything," The benefactor replied. "Name them."

"Bring back all the men who fell," Lesko began. "We fight together or not at all."

"And the second?" the benefactor asked.

"Wipe our memories," Lesko asked. "None of us should know what we really are."

"It shall be done," the benefactor replied.

Lesko smelled a strange smell, his body and mind beginning to grow weak as he slumped to the floor.

"You always live up to your reputation, Lesko," The benefactor said to the waning form. "And every time you win you always request those same two things."

"How..." Lesko struggled. "How many times have we done this?"

"More times than I can count," the benefactor said in an amused tone. "I look forward to your next battle."

Lesko struggled to remain conscious but it was a battle he could not win. He would pass out and for another time in a pile of many, he would have no memory of what had come before.

Two
Minds

Two Minds

The brothers were both technological geniuses that from a young age showed prowess in fields that many adults took years to master. Like any other of their rivalries it seemed that science was unstoppable. They would challenge each other to learn new fields and soon, even at such a young age became masters in many fields. They worked together like no partnership, almost finishing each other's schematics and equations, leaning on each other to learn and boost the other's understanding.

They had invented something amazing, something that they called kinetic water and they were keen to show it off at a science fair at their academy. The competition was fierce as the academy was filled with people their age who were likewise trying to get ahead in science and pushing their knowledge and education to the limit. There were displays of advanced robotics, virtual reality, genetic agriculture, and almost anything the mind could think of.

The brothers stood together as the judges came up. In front of them was a barrel of water, stilling there like any kind of water.

"So, what does this do?" one of the judges asked.

Arin nodded and held an empty bucket upside down above the water. "If I were to get this water to pour into this bucket, what would I have to do?"

"Reverse them," the judge responded. "Lift the water bucket up and pour it into the empty bucket."

"Well, we found another way," Arin declared. "Samuel."

Samuel hit a switch on a control panel he held, and the water instantly began to shift. It rose up as if being poured upside down and soon filled the upside-down bucket in Arin's hand.

"How did you do that?" the judge asked in astonishment. "That is impossible."

"Not impossible," Arin explained. "We circumvent the law of gravity all the time by overpowering it. Every time you pick something up you are using mass and strength to force gravity to temporarily bend. We found an element that can dilute into the water safely and with a type of electromagnet resonance that can manipulate it."

"What looked to you like a pour was up rearranging an electromagnetic field and forcing it up away from one bucket to another."

"We can make it do other things too!" Arin added as Samuel manipulated the controls.

 He slid the bucket off of the water, revealing it in the shape of the bucket, suspended in mid-air.

"The field is completely free form and can do anything we program it to do," Samuel said as he placed a cup on it; the cup not breaking the surface tension. "It can flow like water when we need it to flow and become solid when we need to it to be solid. It could allow someone to have vertical movement up to five thousand feet in the air. We were considering testing it in martial arts, so we can tackle aerial threats."

The judges congratulated the pair and headed off. It was not long until the winners were announced, and the judges eagerly gave it to the brothers. Arin and Samuel were celebrating their win when they saw some scientists in government uniforms. They seemed very interested in the water.

"You realise the second they get a hold of this they are going to patent it and take it from us," Arin commented.

Samuel nodded. "I think we should take it out of here."

"Right," Arin said as he split the water into two containers, giving one to his brother and carrying one on his back.

They grabbed the tablet device and moved out of a side door. The government goons were waiting for them and Arin leapt up off of a chair, jumping over as Samuel slid under.

They led the government goons on a merry chase through the academy, using their intimate knowledge of the layout, soon going toward an outer fire door. Arin dodged through as Samuel hit the button to close it. They both made it through, the door closing just before the goon got to it.

"Sorry, this water is ours!" Arin said with a laugh.

"You want it...you will have to make it yourself," Samuel added.

The Lust for
That at Peace

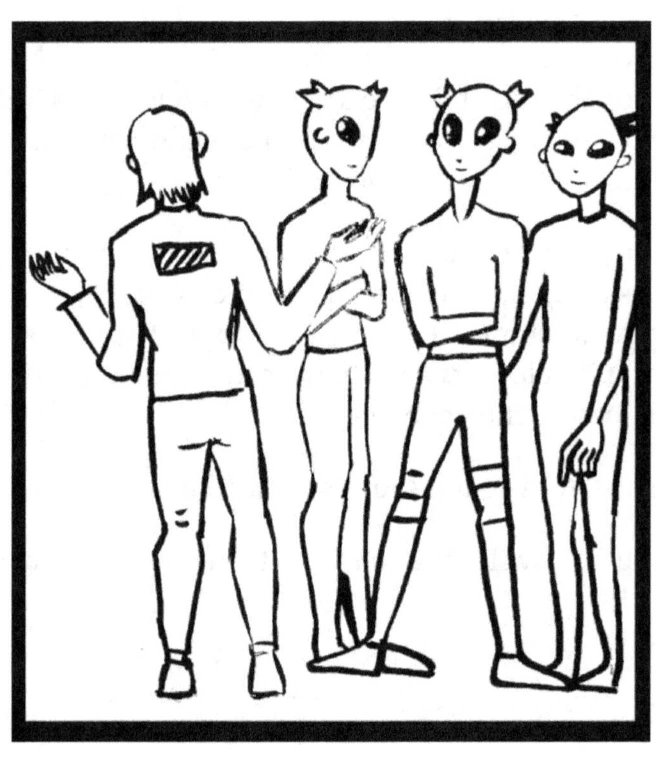

The Lust for That at Peace

On one of the inhabitable worlds the furthest from the earth that man had ever been to a great new colony was formed, and the people there came together to create a great alliance based on trade, tradition and protecting the colony. The colony served the great earth conglomerate but could not often contact them due to the distance. They believed the founding organisation watched over them and their planet and through their strength and wisdom they followed their destiny. They were a proud people with intense customs and ceremonies. They were gifted in agriculture and terraforming, turning barren desert into a paradise for the colony.

Leading the colony was a community leader named Iverson. He had been chosen by the tribes and proven quite proficient and talented in the short time since becoming a leader. Iverson led his people with wisdom and strength, guided by his advisors and the teachings of the core world. The colony and the terraformed farmlands prospered, and the people were happy.

However, in times of peace, there are usually those who would covet the peaceful. There was an exiled mercenary turned pirate named Kerrith, who saw Iverson as unfit and wanted the position for himself. He went to the four corners of the known colony lands, gathering with him every pirate, every scavenger, and all those that felt slighted by the colony and would desire a piece of its power from their own.

Kerrith raised an army and tried to attack the capital of the colony. Iverson led the colony guard and easily repelled them, showing the true might of his army. Kerrith retreated, his forces nearly halved in just one battle. He needed a plan, he needed allies.

Alien tribal warriors made contact with Kerrith. They wanted new lands for their own colony but heard that the leader of the humans did not negotiate easily with aliens...at least not the current one.

Kerrith met with the aliens, making promises for when he would become a leader but told them that he was outnumbered. The aliens had many resources and even more warriors, forming up an army the likes of which the planet had not seen.

Word of the alien's arrival reached Iverson's ears and he knew the danger of taking such a situation too lightly. He sent progression of his own people; those gifted in diplomacy and alien culture, led by his own wife. He decided to reach out with an open hand to these aliens and offer the possibility of trade.

However, the aliens were not knowledgeable of the rituals of the humans and were easily manipulated by Kerrith. Kerrith assured them this was an act of war and that the diplomatic progression was in fact spies.

The aliens and Kerrith's forces ambushed the procession, killing all except for Iverson's wife, whom they captured to use for ransom. They sent word that they were coming to the capital in great numbers. Should they not surrender Iverson's wife would be killed and the city taken by force.

Iverson was faced with a dilemma the likes of which no leader of the colony had ever faced before. Did he put his personal feelings for his wife above the people? Could he risk the people's safety in an act of defiance?

As the aliens and Kerrith marched toward the city in unprecedented numbers. Iverson sent out a call to commune with the earth galactic senate. He asked them for their guidance and the strength to see it through.

The call was brief but the Senate, knowing that they could not intervene in time, knew they had to give him the power since he could not let the colony fall. They granted upon him the title of planetary guardian. Iverson would be the first guardian and work directly with their government to defend the colony.

Iverson went to his people and told them that he would not allow the colony of the far-off planet to fall. Together they formed a defensive strategy that had its best bet to win. Iverson would take a small contingent of special ops soldiers out to confront the oncoming forces.

The small combat team went out and the massive force surrounded them. It was thought that no small group of colony soldiers could withstand the might of the invaders lead by Kerrith. They assumed Iverson would surrender but when they went out to accept it, he signalled his men to attack.

Even surrounded, even outnumbered, the colony soldiers fought in a circle, protecting their ranks, and for every one of them that fell they took fifty of the invaders. Iverson lead them on, inspiring them with his leadership and devotion, the battle taking hours and stretching the invaders to their limit.

However, as more and more of the guard fell it became clear that there were too few to repel them. This was when the other part of Iverson's plan was set in motion.

From all sides they came; groups formed from the bulk of the colony. Soldiers, farmers, regular people stormed the battlefield. They attacked at four places at once, catching the larger forces of the invaders unprepared. Iverson pushed his men on, making the invaders fight from the inside and out.

Soon the bulk of the invader army lay dead, and Iverson confronted Kerrith on the battlefield. He rescued his wife and

Kerrith begged for his life. Iverson looked at the man, seeking to see if he had regret for his actions but saw only jealousy and hate. Kerrith tried to strike at Iverson but was killed before his weapon was even aimed at its target.

The invaders fled, and Iverson reaffirmed the strength of his people. He would be the first of a line of guardians, and whenever the colony was threatened, one of the planetary guardians would be there to defend it.

Gatekeepers

Gatekeepers

In a dangerous age of data theft and corporate espionage, the only real way to get things from one part of the city to the other was via a data courier. Data couriers were like high tech ninjas, able to take and protect people and cargo from thieves no one else could stop. The couriers acted like bodyguards, scouting out around as their clients followed them behind.

There was a festival going on in the city and all of the police and authorities would be focused on it. This would be a good time for industrious thieves to attack, and the scouts and their cash box would be a great target.

The first person to stand in their way was a tall lanky person in tight black clothes. He stood in the challenge as if knowing the couriers were the protectors and the others their charge. The man lit up his suit, a reflective material making it hard for the eye to see. There appeared to be some manner of light reactive panel that somehow tricked the way that the eye perceived movement.

The couriers were confused and struggled to keep up as the man danced between them and looked for a clear shot. However, the couriers had a trick up their sleeve. Being well trained they knew that there was more to combat than what you could see. They focused on hearing and sensing, using those focused senses to override what they were seeing. All it took was one shot to the guy and he was down. With his super thin jumpsuit, he was no match for the courier's strikes.

The couriers knew that if one person was wise to their clients' worth and what they carried then there would be others. People in the underworld of the city talked a lot and when one was slighted, the others would come out of the woodwork quickly.

They had to move fast, knowing if they could get downtown, into a place with lots of people the thieves and others would not be able to get them and likely give up.

Soon the couriers came across three more people. One was small and crouched in the centre as the other two stood over him. They all wore headsets and seemed to be linked together somehow.

The two attackers came after the couriers and their attacks seemed to come from everywhere at once. The couriers tried to counter-attack but found every attack defended...it was like they had eyes in the back of their heads. The couriers, though skilled, could not seem to get past the defence and knew eventually they would tire and make a mistake. They had to focus on a way to overcome their strategy, whatever it was.

This is when one of the couriers came up with it. The attacker in the middle was like a coordinator giving commands to the others. However, that did not quite explain how they could see around. Unless, they were using something else.

The second courier spotted a drone above their heads, and it was a simple matter to take it out. With the eye in the sky gone, the small attacker could not coordinate, and the couriers easily overcame them.

"People are getting trickier and trickier in this city," one of the couriers commented.

"Then we have to be even trickier still!" the other courier replied.

Protectors

Protectors

The brothers made their way through the town, killing some time before what they had to do next. They considered grabbing some food or doing some browsing in the mall. The main problem was to decide which.

Their thoughts were interrupted as they heard some shouting going on down an alley that led to one of the nearby schools. They made their way down the alley to find a group of four high school boys surrounding three younger girls. All were wearing uniforms and seemed to be members of the Fox Scouts.

"Give 'em up," one of the tall boys demanded as he grinned down to one of the scouts. "You guys got the best cookies around and I have a craving."

"Well, we sell them!" one of the scouts said in a defiant tone. "We don't give away our cookies for free...we made these ourselves."

"You should not have made them so good!" another boy shouted. "If you didn't want people to trying to take them, you should not have made them as good as they are."

"That is your lack of self-restraint talking!" the defiant scout retorted. "Do not blame us for your lack of control!"

"We are just five hungry boys!" another high schooler shouted. "So, give us the cookies before we get angry."

"We won't!" the scout replied. "We need these!"

"Well, I would like to know how you are going to stop us!" One of the boys said with a sadistic grin. "You three are no match for us."

"I suppose my brother and I will stop you," Arin replied.

"Yeah, we have seen enough," Samuel added. "We want to buy some of these cookies that apparently are so good, so either buy or buzz off."

The largest of the bullies walked over to Arin and Samuel, towering above them both.

"You guys do not look like fighters to me."

"Oh, is there a dress code to be a badass?" Arin asked. "I will try and coordinate next time."

"Seems the dress code for being a brain-dead bully is sloppy and mismatched," Samuel added. "At least that is what I am taking from all of this."

"Don't make me wipe that smile off of your face!" the bully shouted. "Cuz I will do it."

"You aren't really trying to convince us, are you?" Arin asked. "Studies have shown that a bully's biggest threat is not his prey but the people behind them."

"A bully amongst bullies is like a hungry wolf in a pack of hungry wolves," Samuel added. "Each one of your friends would love to lead your little group, and the moment you show weakness they will take it. The bully will become bullied."

"What the hell are you talking about?" The lead bully asked in disgust and confusion.

"Simple psychiatric anthropology," Arin replied. "The bully is an age-old archetype and we have read up on them much. We know more about this than you do I am afraid."

"Well, what the hell does this psychic anemology have to do with us?" The lead bully asked.

"Well, why don't we do a little experiment?" Arin replied. "Something to see whether or our intensive study versus your brutishness works."

"I have very little faith in your...social science?" the lead bully asked obliviously.

"Well, we can mix in a little physical science too," Samuel replied matter-of-factly. "Because you do not know about our fighting ability, but we can tell you biology. We can strike you somewhere that will be so painful you will never see it coming. It will over-stimulate a specific nerve in your body that will cause more pain than a taser and lay you out for ten times longer than it could. You will be on the ground, struggling for breath and reaching for your comrades to help."

"Their first instinct will be to fight," Arin continued. "But lacking the anatomical knowledge we have they will not know what we did. They will be wracked with fear on how we hurt you and worry that with the slightest step forward we will do to them what we did to you."

Samuel grinned. "This is when doubt will creep into their minds, the doubt that they can help you and they will grasp for straws. All it will take is for one of them to realise that with you hurt and disproven that there will be a power vacuum. All they have to do is be the one to initiate retreat and they are the new leader; leaving you in pain, alone, and at our mercy."

The lead bully looked down at Arin and Samuel. "I suppose that we should just drop this. This is...not really worth our time."

The bullies ran off, eager to get away from the situation they just avoided.

"Could you have done what you said you could do?" one of the three scouts asked. "Could you have hurt them?"

"That and more," Arin replied. "However, it takes a coward to threaten people in a group and all it takes is knowledge to defeat them."

A Small

Distraction

A Small Distraction

The data couriers gathered their clients and moved on. The battles they had fought and the overall feel of the city lately was concerning. There seemed to be some manner of thing behind it. Beyond the simple thugs, beyond the other thieves, there was almost an intelligence to it.

The reason why so many people seemed to find it so easy to ignore the troubles in the city was because it seemed random. People could easily desensitise themselves from threats such as things based on the math of how it worked. It did not matter how many people were hurt as long as the statistic on your individual chances of being part of it was low. It did not matter that a hundred people were attacked in a week as long as you were reasonably unlikely to be one targeted.

The couriers were not so naïve that this would not affect them. Someone was behind the current growth in sophistication of how the underworld was working. All of the high-tech criminals were being helped not only by their gear, but by the complexity of their information. Someone was coordinating them, and the couriers wanted to know who.

The couriers almost had their clients to safety when someone crossed their path. It appeared to be an old woman and she had a mic over her mouth.

"Who are you?" one of the couriers asked. "Why are you blocking our path?"

"I just wish to tell you my tale," The woman began. "Can you not spare but a moment for a woman whose children had left her, whose husband is gone, and who has so very little to fill her days with?"

The couriers felt like they were captivated by the woman's words, as she went on and on they did not feel like fighting; they barely felt like moving.

Another duo came from behind, catching the similarly captivated clients and taking their locked box. The lead courier just watched his body not wanting to do anything. The younger courier fought, moving over and trying to get to the duo as they started to leave. The duo smiled, heading out as fast as they arrived, leaving the couriers and the clients at the mercy of the woman.

The young courier knew that if he did not get control back, they would be done for. The woman had a pair of knives on her hips and could do almost anything to them. The young courier could barely move and knew he would grow more lethargic by the second. He struggled to realise what was going on and realised that it was something hidden in the sound. There was some manner of sonic disrupter that the woman was broadcasting, hiding it within her speech.

The young courier struggled and managed to get his headphones out, putting them in his ears and cranking the music. Immediately he felt better, like whatever was affecting him was losing its grip. He pretended to still be in the thrall of the woman as she came over to him with her knives. The young courier then moved quickly, disabling the audio device the woman had and knocking her out.

Instantly the others recovered, and the young courier moved in chase of the duo. They caught up with them a few blocks later. They were not fighters, relying on the woman to do their dirty work. The courier quickly defeated them and returned the property. Shortly, the couriers delivered their clients to their destination; left wondering who was helping the underworld flourish and grow stronger in the shadows.

Broken but Stronger

Broken but Stronger

It had been many generations since the colony world had been established. History tells that the world used to be part of a massive space alliance government. Humans, aliens and other peoples all together to form a grand society where all could prosper.

This is where the history becomes divergent. Some speak of a massive calamity that befell the world, others talk of civil wars, some of the clan difference. Whatever happened, this massive government and the ones that formed it are long gone. The world has become primal, dangerous, and untamed once again.

Many of the races that had once been part of the world have either fled underground or were gone forever. The main factions of the planet that inhabited the surface were humans and aliens.

The aliens were one of the stronger races and one of the only ones actually prepared for whatever happened to the surface. They chose some lands, fortified them, and held on to what they had. They focused on survival and became very suspicious of outsiders. They shut their borders and beyond what they controlled they cared not what happened in the world, only venturing out in times of need for resources.

The humans were not prepared but proved much more formidable than the others. They formed a new nomadic society that weeded out the weak and made the strong stronger. They readopted the tribal state, strong warriors gathering together for the greater good of those around them. They inhabited the lands near the aliens but knew all too well that they were not to mess with them.

It had been so long since the humans and aliens separated, there were some that did not believe the other existed anymore.

Both societies had a strong belief in the origin planets they came from. They believed that the home planets had stopped listening, forsaking the world and those on it. The aliens believed it was a test. The home planet wanted to see if they were worthy before they decided to return them to their former glory. The humans cursed the home planet government, desiring to find power for themselves to do what needed to be done. Some believed that soon, through hard work, that they would become like those that came before and go to seek them and take the world back.

Though two beliefs differed, but both were forged by the times around them and both believed that they were on their own.

There were some, believers, who thought the home planet governments were not gone; that they were indeed still listening and watching. Though the world had become primordial and savage, there was still much there untapped, and one does not leave such a treasure unattended, especially with those who did not know what they had in command of it.

The originators would come back, reclaim the world, and it would be hell on those who still lived below them.

Taste by
Design

Taste by Design

Arin and Samuel ate the squirrel scout cookies, both shocked with how very good they were.

"These cookies are truly amazing," Arin commented. "I must admit I have never had anything like them before."

"What is your secret?" Samuel asked. "I can almost not help myself with these."

"Well, we might have stumbled across a thing with a really dark past," Tamara began. "You see in a war many years ago there was this group that the soldiers could not stop. They fought them and fought them but as hard as they tried, they could not make a dent in them. They decided that they needed to break the rules and poison them. They managed to get some poison in the water supply that had a limited time before it diluted. However, the first few enemies that drank it noticed the horrific taste of the poison and warned the others. It was a failure.

"However, the ones that drank it did not die, but became lethargic and easy to overcome and capture. They decided that they should try again. The scientists did tests to find the exact nerve points on the tongue that told the body and brain something was something that had to be eaten. They found a chemical that stimulated a response and made the body want it. They then added it to the water supply and boom...almost all of the enemy forces drank it, passed out, and were captured."

"After the war, people wondered how to use it," Trishae continued. "However, the problem was that people would want it a lot and eat it a lot but the chemical, though harmless, had a point where it would hit the body and then do the opposite; becoming disgusting and making the eater reject it. They could not find the balance and gave up on it."

"This is where we came in," Arianna chimed in. "We found the recipe in an old textbook and recreated it. We did some tests and found the exact variance to where the body likes it and when it hates it. We figured out how long it takes for the body to want it again and from there we calculated the exact number of ideal cookies per week someone should eat. We mixed in other harmless additives to dilute it and delay it a bit and got it right, so the average person can eat up to two boxes a week and love it without a backlash. We track all of our sales and strive to not sell more boxes to one person within that time."

"Then there are family consumption rates," Tamara pointed out. "We have it all figured out."

"So, you have it so people will develop a strong loyalty to it without addiction or a backlash?" Arin asked in shock. "You are geniuses."

"When we combine our efforts, we are," Tamara said with a smile. "Simple chemistry, math, and an understanding of human nature."

"People have done a lot more with a lot less," Arin replied.

About The Author

Ralph K Jones is an Australian author and storyteller whose works serve as a contemporary response to primeval human truths. His inspiration comes from real-life experiences, ancient tales and daily ethical dilemmas, which he rewrites and transforms into futuristic Sci-fi and dystopian stories. While the stories have clear messages, Ralph is determined not to tell his readers what to think. His writing took off after the birth of his first child when he would write down the stories he told her at night, so in future, his other children could enjoy the same tales in the future 600 stories later, and his children are now growing up fast it's time to share these adventures with the world.

A firm believer in individuality, he hopes that he can encourage people to think for themselves—going against the herd and doing what is right, not merely what's expected. His writing demonstrates an adoration and respect for the human experience, which Ralph believes has remained fundamentally unchanged at its core. Through stories, let there be no doubt people can share lessons and help each other. You can visit him online at **www.ralphkjones.com** or on Twitter (**@RalphKJones**).

Continue Your Journey

Further must read collections from Ralph K Jones include:

QUANTUM ENTANGLEMENT VOLUMES ONE TO FOURTEEN, SIXTEEN TO TWENTY-ONE

ETHICAL DISPLACEMENT

FUNDAMENTAL MATTER

GRAVITATIONAL MOMENTUM

GENETIC INHERITANCE VOLUMES ONE TO TWO

THORIUM HALF LIFE VOLUMES ONE TO FOUR

ANTHROPIC PRINCIPLES VOLUMES ONE TO SIX

QUANTUM ATTRACTION VOLUMES ONE TO SIX

QUANTUM AWAKENING VOLUMES ONE TO TWELVE

www.ingramcontent.com/pod-product-compliance
Lightning Source LLC
Chambersburg PA
CBHW071457150726
48000CB00006B/2597